SCATALOG
A Kid's Field Guide to Animal Poop

HOW TO TRACK
AN ELEPHANT

Henry Owens

"BECAUSE EVERYBODY POOPS"

WINDMILL
BOOKS
New York

Published in 2014 by Windmill Books, An Imprint of Rosen Publishing
29 East 21st Street, New York, NY 10010

First Edition

Editor: Amelie von Zumbusch
Photo Research: Katie Stryker
Book Design: Colleen Bialecki

Photo Credits: Cover (top) travelphoto/Shutterstock.com; cover (bottom) Richard du Toit/Gallo Images/ Getty Images; p. 5 Henry Wrenn/Shutterstock.com; p. 6 Mohamed El Hebeishy/Shutterstock.com; pp. 8, 13, 22 Four Oaks/Shutterstock.com; pp. 9, 16 Villers Steyn/Shutterstock.com; p. 11 Fuse/Thinkstock.com; p. 12 Steve Bower/Shutterstock.com; p. 15 Tish1/Shutterstock.com; p. 17 (top left) Anan Kaewkhammul/ Shutterstock.com; p. 17 (top right) Steffen Foerster/Shutterstock.com; p. 17 (bottom left) John Michael Evan Potter/Shutterstock.com; p. 17 (center right) MartinMaritz/Shutterstock.com; p. 17 (bottom right) K&D Foster Photographers/Shutterstock.com; p. 18 Jlri Haureljuk/Shutterstock.com; p. 19 Andrew Plumptre/ Oxford Scientific/Getty Images; p. 21 Andrzej Gibasiewicz/Shutterstock.com.

Library of Congress Cataloging-in-Publication Data

Owens, Henry.
   How to track an elephant / by Henry Owens.
      pages cm. — (Scatalog: a kid's field guide to animal poop)
   Includes index
   ISBN 978-1-61533-887-0 (library) — ISBN 978-1-61533-893-1 (pbk.) —
   ISBN 978-1-61533-899-3 (6-pack)
   1. Elephants—Juvenile literature. 2. Animal droppings—Juvenile literature. I. Title.
   QL737.P98O945 2014
   599.67—dc23
                               2013028404

Manufactured in the United States of America

CPSIA Compliance Information: Batch # BW14WM: For Further Information contact Windmill Books, New York, New York at 1-866-478-0556

CONTENTS

WATCH YOUR STEP

Have you ever seen an African elephant at the zoo? African elephants are the largest land animals on Earth. Finding an elephant in the wild is not as easy as you might think, though. One of the best ways to track, or find, an elephant is by looking for its poop!

Scientists use elephant poop to count the number of elephants in an area. Safari guides can use poop to find an elephant's path and follow it. If you ever find yourself in elephant **habitat**, watch your step. You wouldn't want to step in the huge piles of poop that these large animals produce.

As you can see, this African elephant is pooping. Elephant poop is also known as dung. Elephants can produce 240 pounds (109 kg) of dung each day!

WHERE TO FIND ELEPHANTS

There are two **species**, or types, of elephants. Asian elephants live in the forests and grasslands of India and Southeast Asia. African elephants live in the parts of Africa that lie south of the Sahara.

These elephants live on a savanna in Uganda. Some scientists divide the African elephants living in savannas and forests into two separate species.

Many African elephants live in **savannas**. A savanna is a kind of grassland with few trees or bushes. Other African elephants live in warm, wet **rain forests**. Thick trees block much of the sunlight from reaching the rain forest floor. This makes it hard to see animals, even those as large as elephants. That makes poop extra useful when you are tracking elephants in a rain forest.

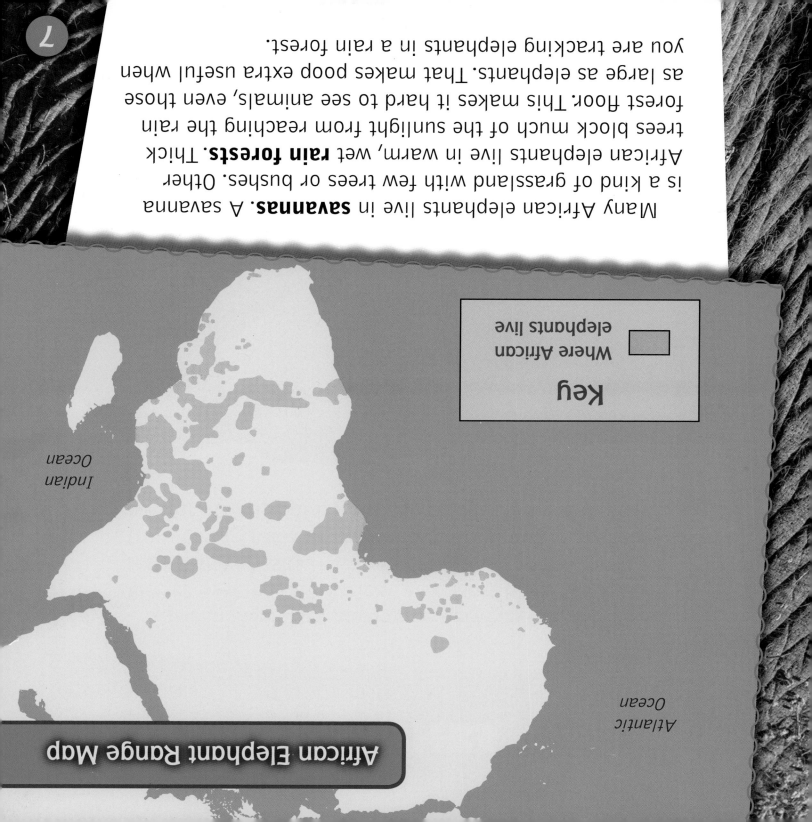

African Elephant Range Map

Key

Where African elephants live

Atlantic Ocean

Indian Ocean

TUSKS AND TRUNKS

African elephants grow to be between 8.2 and 13 feet (2.5–4 m) tall. African elephants have two long teeth called **tusks.** They use their tusks to pull bark from trees. Trackers know that trees that are pushed over or stripped of bark mean elephants were there.

Male elephants, or bulls, are the largest. African elephant bulls can weigh as much as 15,000 pounds (6,804 kg).

An elephant's trunk is a very useful feature. This long nose is used for more than just breathing. Two fingerlike points on the end let the elephant pick up a piece of fruit as small as a marble. Elephants sometimes drag their trunks on the ground, leaving marks that trackers follow.

Elephants drink by sucking water up into their trunks and then squirting it into their mouths.

SPEAKING ELEPHANT

Elephants are very social animals. Female elephants live in groups called **herds** with other females and their young. Male elephants usually live alone or with other males.

Elephants use their bodies and voices to **communicate** with each other. A folded ear or a curled trunk can tell the herd to move in a certain direction or that danger is near. Elephants often wrap their trunks around each other as a greeting or a hug. They make roars, screams, and trumpeting noises. When tracking an elephant, listen for these loud sounds.

The leader of an elephant herd is known as the matriarch. The matriarch tends to be the oldest elephant in the herd.

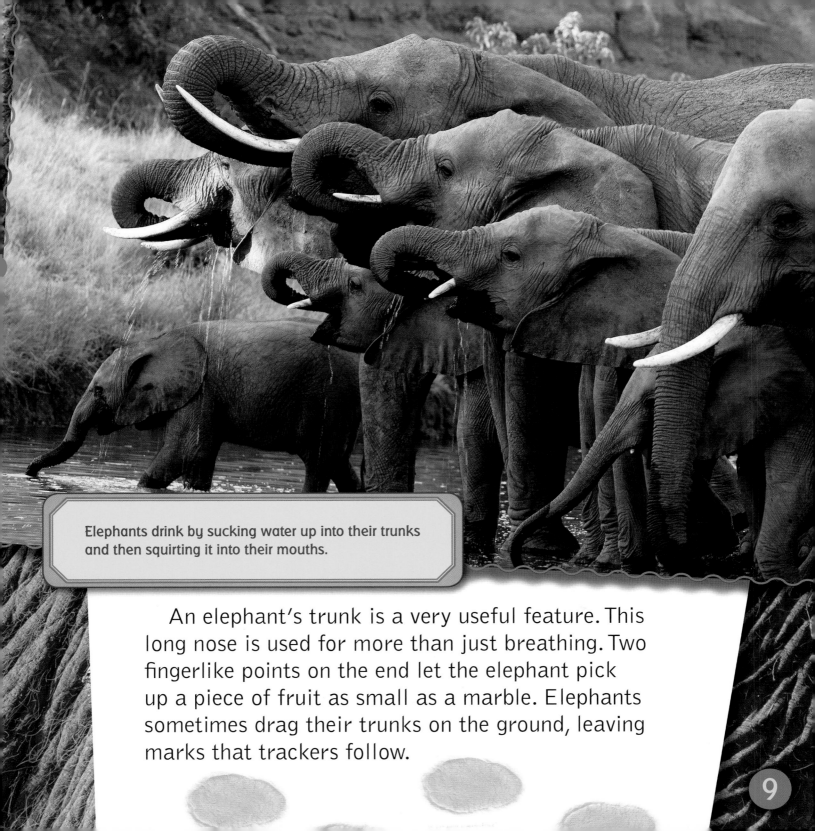

Elephants drink by sucking water up into their trunks and then squirting it into their mouths.

An elephant's trunk is a very useful feature. This long nose is used for more than just breathing. Two fingerlike points on the end let the elephant pick up a piece of fruit as small as a marble. Elephants sometimes drag their trunks on the ground, leaving marks that trackers follow.

9

SPEAKING ELEPHANT

Elephants are very social animals. Female elephants live in groups called **herds** with other females and their young. Male elephants usually live alone or with other males.

Elephants use their bodies and voices to **communicate** with each other. A folded ear or a curled trunk can tell the herd to move in a certain direction or that danger is near. Elephants often wrap their trunks around each other as a greeting or a hug. They make roars, screams, and trumpeting noises. When tracking an elephant, listen for these loud sounds.

The leader of an elephant herd is known as the matriarch. The matriarch tends to be the oldest elephant in the herd.

GROWING UP IN THE HERD

When a baby elephant is born, it is already about 3 feet (1 m) tall and can weigh more than 200 pounds (91 kg). Young elephants are called calves. A female elephant will give birth to a new calf every two to four years.

Like most young animals, elephant calves like to play!

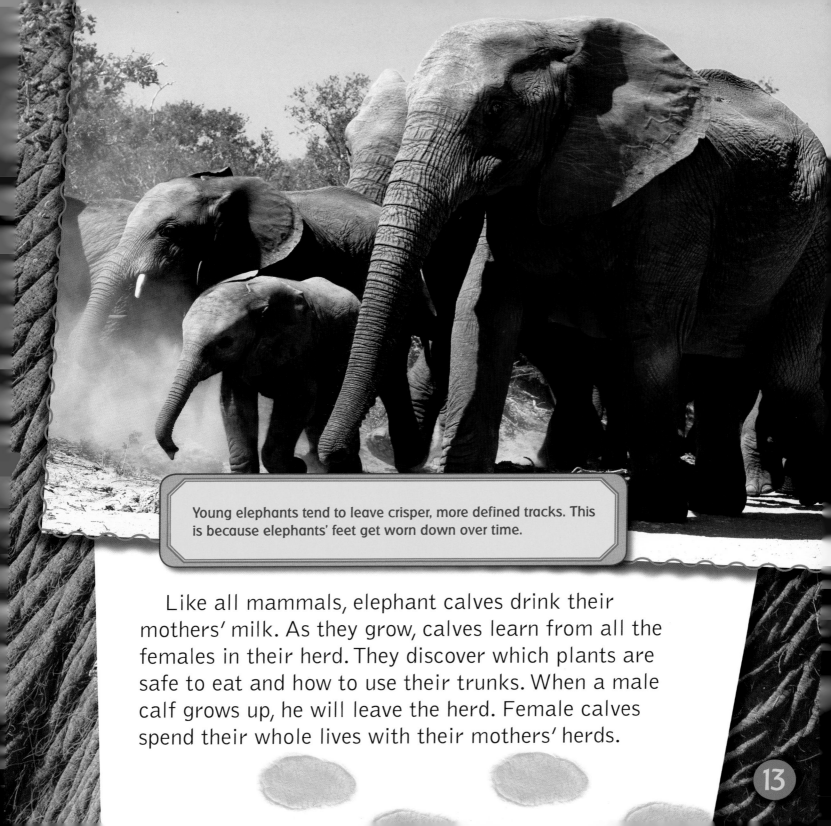

Young elephants tend to leave crisper, more defined tracks. This is because elephants' feet get worn down over time.

Like all mammals, elephant calves drink their mothers' milk. As they grow, calves learn from all the females in their herd. They discover which plants are safe to eat and how to use their trunks. When a male calf grows up, he will leave the herd. Female calves spend their whole lives with their mothers' herds.

BIG ANIMALS, BIG APPETITES

African elephants are **herbivores**. This means that they eat only plants. Each day, elephants roam over large distances looking for grasses, leaves, roots, bark, and fruit to eat. Elephants have to eat huge amounts of food to get the energy they need.

ELEPHANT DIGESTIVE SYSTEM

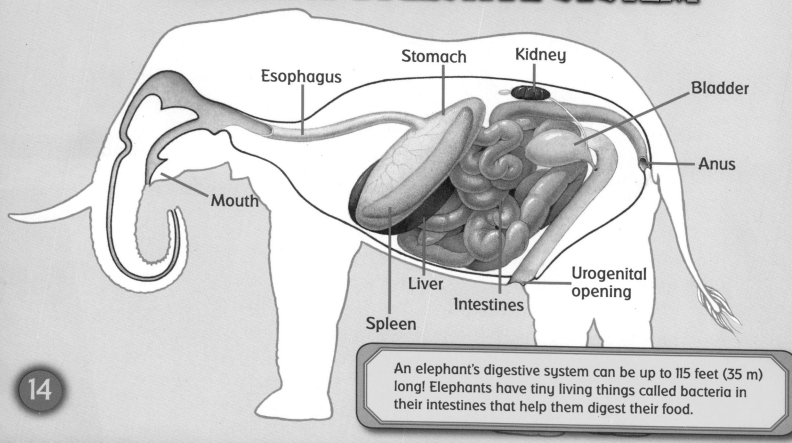

Esophagus

Stomach

Kidney

Bladder

Mouth

Anus

Liver

Urogenital opening

Intestines

Spleen

An elephant's digestive system can be up to 115 feet (35 m) long! Elephants have tiny living things called bacteria in their intestines that help them digest their food.

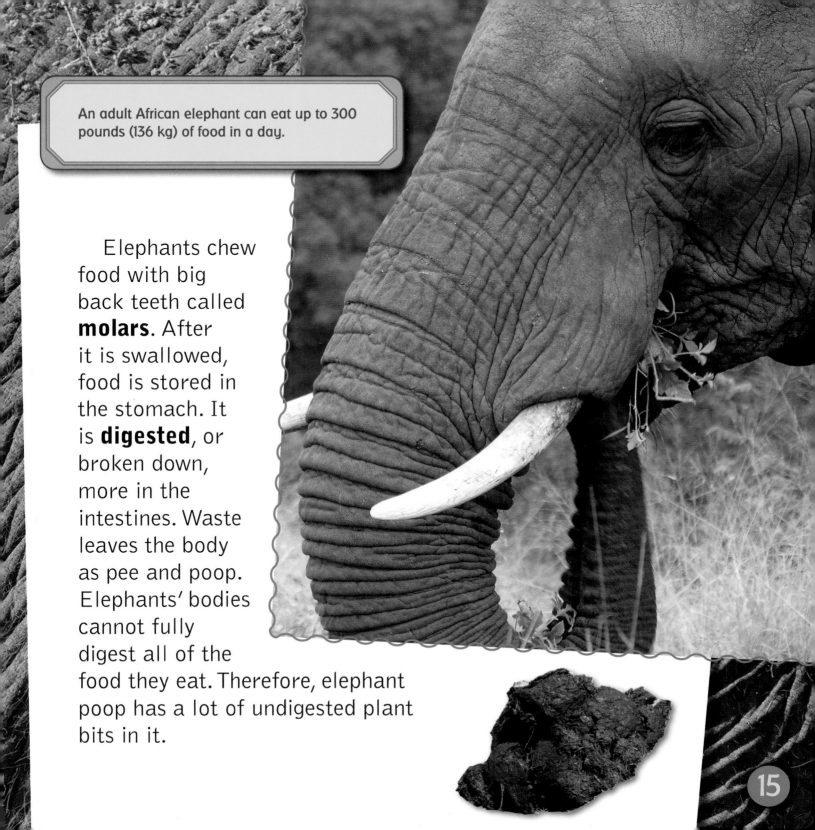

An adult African elephant can eat up to 300 pounds (136 kg) of food in a day.

Elephants chew food with big back teeth called **molars**. After it is swallowed, food is stored in the stomach. It is **digested**, or broken down, more in the intestines. Waste leaves the body as pee and poop. Elephants' bodies cannot fully digest all of the food they eat. Therefore, elephant poop has a lot of undigested plant bits in it.

USEFUL POOP

Since so much of it is undigested food, elephant poop has a lot of **nutrients** in it. Nutrients are things that living things need to stay alive and grow. Many animals, such as warthogs and monkeys, eat elephant dung. Elephant calves sometimes even eat their mothers' poop.

Can you see the pieces of undigested grass in this elephant dung?

THINGS THAT RELY ON ELEPHANT DUNG

Mushrooms: The nutrients in dung make it perfect for both mushrooms and plants to grow out of.

Baboons: Baboons and other animals dig through dung to find seeds and insects to eat.

Cape Spurfowl: The Cape spurfowl is one of many birds that eat elephant dung.

Dung Beetles: Poop is the main food for dung beetles. Some kinds make balls in which to store food or lay eggs.

Elephant Calves: Calves get bacteria that help them digest food into their stomachs when they eat dung.

Elephant dung also helps spread plant seeds. When an elephant eats a plant, the seeds are released in its poop. As the elephant roams, plants are able to spread to new places. Humans have found other ways to use elephant poop, too. People use it as **fertilizer** to help plants grow. It can even be used to make paper.

TRACKING TIPS

Finding an elephant's poop lets you know that an elephant has been in the area. It can tell you much more, too. Elephant dung can give you an idea of the size and age of the elephant that produced it. It can also tell you whether the elephant is a male or a female and what it has been eating.

Elephants have big footprints. Their front feet leave round tracks. Their back feet leave oval tracks, such as those seen here.

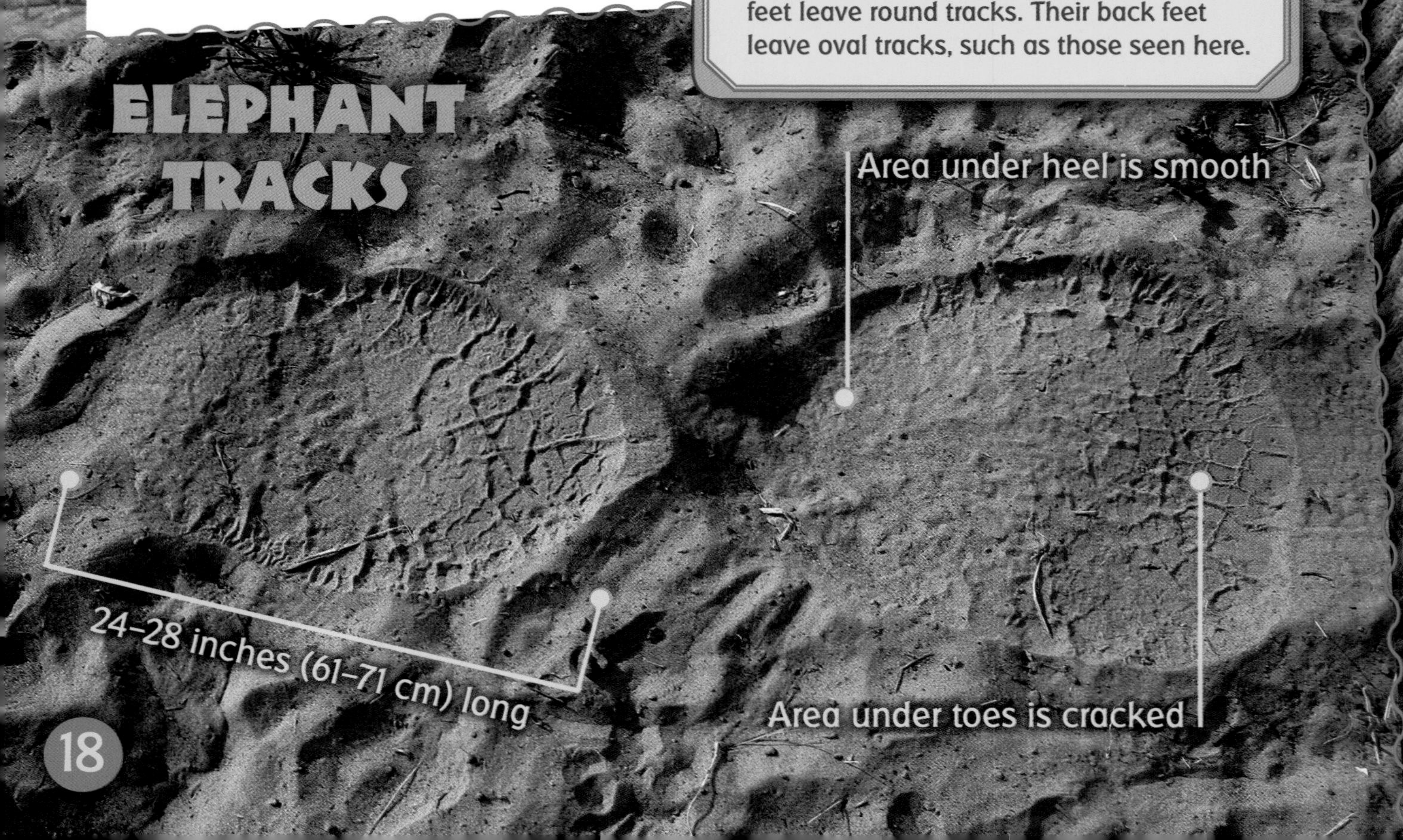

ELEPHANT TRACKS

Area under heel is smooth

24–28 inches (61–71 cm) long

Area under toes is cracked

These park rangers are putting a radio collar on an elephant. Radio collars help people keep track of where elephants are at all times.

There are other ways to track elephants, too. Safari guides look for footprints and marks that show an elephant was dragging its trunk on the ground. They also look for water holes dug near rivers and listen for the sound of breaking branches.

ELEPHANTS IN DANGER

A little over 100 years ago, millions of elephants roamed Africa. Today, there are about 500,000 African elephants in the wild. For many years, elephants were killed for their ivory tusks, which were very valuable. Laws were passed to stop the sale of ivory. However, ivory is still popular in some parts of the world, and **poachers** continue to hunt elephants.

Another major threat to elephants is habitat loss. Many people are trying to help elephants by setting aside land in national parks for them to live on. Today, nearly 13,000 elephants live in Tsavo National Park, in Kenya.

These elephants live in South Africa's Addo Elephant National Park. The park is home to more than 500 elephants and to many other animals, too.

KEEPING ELEPHANTS SAFE

Tracking and finding elephants can be a lot of fun. It is incredible to see them living in the wild!

Tracking elephants helps keep them safe, too. Scientists in Africa use GPS collars to learn where elephants are and where they are going. If an elephant gets too close to a farm, rangers can stop it before it eats a farmer's crops. This is just one way that tracking helps elephants and people live together peacefully!

Many animals and plants depend on elephant dung. It is important to keep these intelligent, interesting animals around.

GLOSSARY

communicate (kuh-MYOO-nih-kayt) To share facts or feelings.

digested (dy-JEST-ed) Broke down food so that the body can use it.

fertilizer (FUR-tuh-lyz-er) Something put in soil to help crops grow.

habitat (HA-buh-tat) The kind of land where an animal or a plant naturally lives.

herbivores (ER-buh-vorz) Animals that eat only plants.

herds (HURDZ) Groups of the same kind of animal living together.

molars (MOH-lurz) Large back teeth used for grinding up food.

nutrients (NOO-tree-ents) Food that a living thing needs to live and grow.

poachers (POH-cherz) People who illegally kill animals that are protected by the law.

rain forests (RAYN FOR-ests) Thick forests that receive a large amount of rain during the year.

savannas (suh-VA-nuz) Grasslands with few trees or bushes.

species (SPEE-sheez) One kind of living thing. All people are one species.

tusks (TUSKS) Long, large pointed teeth that come out of the mouths of some animals.

INDEX

WEBSITES

For web resources related to the subject of this book, go to:
www.windmillbooks.com/weblinks and select this book's title.